NORTHWOODS

- Taxus -

NORTHWOODS

Peter Dent

NORTHWOODS

First edition 1992
© Peter Dent 1992
All rights reserved

ISBN 1 873012 26 8 (*paperback*)
ISBN 1 873012 27 6 (*hardback*)

Cover design by Caroline Allsup-Evans
© 1992

ACKNOWLEDGEMENTS
Some of these poems were first published in *Ninth Decade, Northward Journal* (Ontario), *Outposts, Tears In The Fence*, and *Westwords*. Others appeared in *Midwinter Nights* (Oasis Books). To all the editors concerned my grateful thanks.

Published by
TAXUS PRESS
at Stride
37 Portland Street
Exeter
Devon EX1 2EG
England

Contents

NORTHWOODS

Wings, dark seed. Winter.
John Riley

NORTHWOODS

I

By night an atmosphere. Each time he closed his eyes. Not one he'd sought to generate. But still it came, in light and scent: woods, to the north, a fierce cold air. And something in the blood.

At twilight, dustings of snow he'd find on green in shadow. Falls unseen. At times, the car he'd waited for, its headlights reaching out ahead. A long, ascending road that vanished into trees.

Rapidity of day and night, a feature. Almost a blur, yet every image curiously sharp. That deer he once made out against the trees. Its frozen turn. An eye in bright, almost surreal clarity.

Rapidity of day and night. Both here and elsewhere. Yet his mind could find no access to the seasons, feel their pull on energy and will. No sense at all of movement, fever in the herd, ice breaking, pollen issuing in cloud.

Confusion every vapour trail that entered, crossed the blue. While nights, the nights he travelled, saw no interruption. The single constant registering in his life. Continuum where he must suffer, cleanse infected wounds. Its sterile pause.

Still life. An alien, unapproachable calm. Exceptions only in his breath, a virus, yellow eye of the questing lamp.

II

Pinewoods. Their silent breathing fills his night of sleeplessness. Eyes closed, he watches, knows their endless journeys in a white-flaked wind.

No owls, no wolves. No cars on the ice-packed road that curves back south. The way he came. Retreat of trees, each side, in the rising moon. No more than yards.

It's only the early hours make real headway: pre-dawn greys that breach a black opacity. A time he finds himself the more awake, his senses tingling, readying for day.

An endless sighing, 4 a.m. That maze of trackways opens up, but every
one he's seen and tried before. A sliding moon that finds him chipping
ice from day, no saving thought where one should run.

III
Fine tilth of dark, an even spread of gold. These living trees a gang puts
to the saw - the clearing made in hours.

Cupped hands that feel the cold lift out a mound that has no weight at
all. Blue smoking fires, worlds emptying so easily.

A swarm of wood ants looks to rearrange the glade. Hands to the
flames. Magnesium flaring, white cloud racing overhead.

IV
Metallic green was how he once saw time. Its clockwork.

Now, with age, he finds that years are other: how their late, accelerating
pace is contradicted by the way they draw in distance, things remote...
disputing ownership and sequence. A minimal infinity where edges
never quite fade out.

Absurdities like these he cannot altogether put aside. His mind become
a crucible. Its workings frequently a maelstrom, something he must
live with.

Every night he smells the scent of hacked wood on his hands,
discovering stickiness beneath the nails. And dreams of amber in the
soft flood of his lamp. Obsessive images that call and call, shift-
working to some other scale.

V
He seeks a pause before the day begins. The trunk he leans against still
drips with last night's rain. A softness underfoot.

There are letters to write, perhaps too many. He thinks of words and the
desperation of silence, but cannot tell which voice he'll raise today.

A camouflage is found: an early light that hides as much as it reveals.
The glade he walks to gleams, but there is no way in. A wall of sleet
hangs virgin as the page.

VI

Order of light, a pointing of seasons: treeful of cones.

How much is overlooked: between the shadows of trunks: each time the
pupil's forced to change, contract. Snow-blind to everything that leaves
the dark. See these few pieces, out of greenwoods,

how they pause. Mid-point of lives, a fulcrum. See them fall.

VII

A clutter of fern and woodchips underfoot, the unsuspected, ankle-
breaking log. No easy going where he searched. Thin light, unbroken
cloud. A slope that turned its grey face north. Was this the place?

Together, thirty years before, they'd climbed to pitch camp high above a
valley road, a stony stream. Two nights they'd slept in a grove of pines,
their primus seeing off the cold. Now, when he turned, made out that
angle of opposing ridges, he was sure. He paused for what seemed
hours. Dark speck to those below.

Renewal, reconciliation.... he couldn't put his finger on the word. That
he was back was good, perhaps enough. Something demanded. Yet had
he not, consistently, put off the day? No answers there, or none that
came to hand. A stillness, everywhere the racing cloud.

Around him, almost lost in debris of the former wood, new saplings
struggled for the light. Seed of an earlier generation. On their way. One
question though: how many woods had grown before and since? It came
to him but failed to make much sense. In time what care he'd lavish on
ideas of conservation.

Zig-zagging down the slope, he smiled to think how crazed or drunk he
looked, avoiding each new fragile growth. Three times he fell. Face
glowing, glasses, in a gust of wind and rain, exciting everything to
light: the mildest greys, the fading off-white distances of space. How

long it took, the drop.

But time in hand, one sapling that he'd suddenly, impulsively, wrenched free. Its roots in everything he knew. A rehabilitation. Now he knew the word. A life he'd carry home and nurture, confident its simple form could redescribe the sky, its endless vacant glare.

VIII

Dark canopy of trees. And a rocky outcrop, single streaming eye. The eye he watches now as every day across the gulf.

And notes the fine decay of seasons, modulating colours of his world. A self-imposed retreat, demands his own. What else enjoined?

By dusk the cloud envelops. Distances by steps expand. No record of the hours in what he brings himself to do.

The eye stares inward. Everything is curdled there like stars: his manufactures, journeyings, emotions.

Wisps of shadow slip into a pool of dark. The background words he frets on soon eroding to a sigh.

IX

Beside the house half-broken branches dip into a pool and sway. The logs cut yesterday now gather frost. Light fades.

Already he's rehearsed his list a dozen times. Provisioning for Winter takes both time and nerve. No sign again of the truck someone had said would call, voice crackling down the line.

Only the one road that could reach him, ice always a hazard on its slow ascent. Anxiety, white sky and breath. He rings again but can't get through. Soon dark, the house lights on.

And hours pass by uncounted. Somehow, somewhere his list is wrong. An entry missed, perhaps an unintentional change, a slip of the pen. Who knows?

Through glass he makes out roundels - water, wood and smoke. His
floating backwoods life. Unchanged. Nowhere to move.

X
Clearings, green oases where the mind is free to drift.

He thinks of them, deep in the shadows of his panelled rooms.

A photograph of lilies in the post, black-framed.

Another friend emerges smiling into dream.

XI
No need to look, to search. His skin is sensitive enough to tell when

mists arise, unravelling through trees, or midges choose to generate
their storms.

Identities he values, essences: distinct, observable, with no reliable
location. Such as can, at times, be guaranteed.

So much to tell, to explain. The mysteries of his laughter, opaline,
across an autumn glade.

XII

1

Through rime the forest lifts its dark
geometry. Half-buried logs
                    are cracked with frost.

2

By night and day he carries wood.
A shadow where they intersect.
                    His secret time.

3

A red flame licks about his mind,
is lost again engaging cold.
                  No thought stays whole.

CODEX

There was green, good green to be found. The ice which midnight brought was disappearing fast. Little more than a surface wafer kept him back. Soon dawn would crackle over oak and fern. If only he could keep himself in check, sustain a welcome for that first improbable delight.

For days his whereabouts had been a mystery. A cave within a cave? He scarcely knew himself. For sure, no chance of explanations that would stick. All he recalled was a spectrum tampered with, its missing seventh. A world that boiled and froze alternately. No order there informing growth, sweet sap to give light back its vivid play - inventiveness, a leaf on stem, the stem on root.

For days no green at all had sung itself into his mind. He'd waited, prayed, established pacts with every shadow in the house, with every gleam that came to rest. Night after night an absence dawn would cruelly confirm, then sleep that overwhelmed him, scarred his mind.

The hour, perhaps, now come, his fingers brushed the last cold rivulets away. Those crystal myriads he'd known, mosaic eyes of dream, his mind's kaleidoscope, gave way to single, credible impressions: lifting and falling light, intensities that had him reaching out to touch. Almost like flying, his eyelid wings cleared darkened fields, made parallels with far off glisterings. The palette waited in his hand, assured of substance, everything he wished.

The first viridian, when it came, came quickly, took his breath away. It brushed against his hand like dust or pollen, settled. Filling and deepening. Tones paler and brighter followed. A keen autumnal Spring, a wood that gave itself to flood. No palette ran as vigorously with vine and leaf. What always slipped away before now came to him. His long-lost Nordic labyrinth.

Incredibly, he felt its arms around him, pulled them tight. The wood was his. No further need to occupy that bleached-out world, his past, extract coherences where there were none. His senses filled and swayed with green, its rhythms issuing in fronds that knew a subtler light...

Whose way was paint, whose legends underwrote a planing of reality, the boundary he skimmed. A little *Kells* in making, twenty pages, spiral-bound, its self-willed panic intertwining themes of time and growth and colour, and calling out for more than artless reverie. For signallings instead - to forces that might lift the mind. Crescendoes where the old observable realities give way to new, or rather deepen, merge into some greater whole.

His sketchbook life worked out in hours. Strict sequence, numbered. And with nothing left to chance: each page awarded names. The names the ancients found for vital energies. His presence like a colour, breathing through the whole. At one. At last. A restless peace whose tendrils, hands link up and dare not fall. A resonance through watchers' fingertips, fierce and fragile, green.

FORESTS

A movement between the trees, a redness travelling the eye. Out there?
Or do we speak again of mind, of things too quick to grasp?

Where they go the forest deepens, lit by twilight only, blue and shifting
shadows. A consciousness to fill, we do not own. But no one there, it
seems,

no witnesses to docile words, their dark bouquet. A life that's closed,
closed in, all voices one. The day, our simple traffic, brings us through.

On every world encountered there's our seal. Whose seal? Such *our-ness*
being what we share, good neighbours, finds the glade, and every dash
of red

holds good. Good words, look where the trees were clawed. Long tears
and other wilder signs. Great monuments and verses where we find or
lose our-

selves, eyes bright with fear. What moves to make, what sequences of
rapid fire. A golden resin trickles hour by hour. It's life that catches
under nails.

SPACE

Half-light, a pause. He watches mist edge into woods, dissolve, a half-smile on his lips. An hour from dreams, he tries to make it all connect: events like overloaded trees, tier after broken tier.

The canvas waits contentedly for form, the linearity of his mind. How practice shapes, years coming into play. Immodestly he calls them up.

Remote and near, an interchangeability. Subtle space he gives the unexpected, mysteries of the real. Cloud order.

Beyond his hands, the fir-cones fall at random, punctuate an hour. His artful narrative evolves. Off-whites and greys, the sleepy background tones pervade. Hide and pervade.

CONNECTIONS

Someone is calling. Over grey-green leaves, their coarseness, run unbroken lines. My mind is quietly intimate with space. The phone that no one answers offers all we need to know.

The afternoon so still. I dream of thought that slows and slows. Sub-zero, and the branches blacken against the sky. The eye is a glitter. Every crack the sun can't reach is sealed.

Inaudible today, the leaves at rest. How many are we, that the intervals still stand? The phone stops ringing, shadows ripple after cloud. The roots spread out beneath us even as we speak.

INTERVAL

The dawn is wherever the dawn waits. Unseasonal weather is becoming the norm. I am not alone in seeing out the night.

A gleam travels between houses. And nothing, not even the wind will intervene. Easy to discover absolutes, less easy to reason with them.

All those who cannot wait for words are taking the short cut. Threading freighters on a skyline, one by one, until it greys.

APPROACH

Late Summer. Every flower lies broken in the frost. No petal stirs and we can't speak. Around us children learn to scream.

The eye can barely take it, colour denser than before. It's light that brings us here, its textures brim.

All movement meets the eye, but there are other frequencies. Come closer, fall, and let the words that matter freeze.

LANDFALL

I

Dropping from a straggle of pines on the seaward hill. And down,
across a clear blue gulf to town, to a curtain's russet fold. A place to
settle. This wasp and a half, our Horntail, emblem of the woods
(though there are none left whole). Frightener of adult and child alike,
but harmless, seeking out decay, the furtherance of its vivid line. More
than an hour its urgency and poise excite our care. Till younger voices
steal away. A jam jar emptied, rinsed and dried to seal its future, see it
free.

II

Cold sky to the north. A window on the Rhine, near Koblenz, framed
again by a dark wood mirror. A glitter as the barges glide in left and
right. Line overlapping line, crisp black and white, the other colours
dulled. No sounds of water reach the hotel room, though the current's
fast and banks are briefly, seriously awash after a week of rain. A creak
of floorboards from above and to each side is all one hears. Guests in
and out, criss-crossing lives that make for rapid conversation in the
lounge. How everyone at length observes the awkwardness of foreign
keys, their weight. The numbered silver always out of sight. Brief focus
on the landing stage where some make tracks for home, where strange
lights flare.

III

Anonymous the postcard, sender known. Without a placename, stamp.
No postmark, and not a single word to give the game away. An estuary
suffused in pre-dawn blues, fog drifting at a curve of light. But
something now to ponder on - what seems like broken ice fragmenting,
topped with snow. Perhaps a Finnish landscape. Winter breaking into
Spring, the unseen wolves retreating north. But then, her travels never
reached that far; too keen on closer lands, their well-lit capitals and
worked-out myths. Light pre-arranged, the matter, all she finds, already
come to hand.

IV

Beach littered once again. A current moved to frenzy by some distant gale. Drums, ropes, a hundred plastics in the man-made tide: two lines of flotsam where the waves advance. How frequently we're told to leave suspicious things alone, or where to watch for them. White stencil over blue, black stencil over red. Their nursery colours cannot fail to catch the eye. Containers sealed, unreadable. The worst found wearing hieroglyphs of rust. Words gone and uniformed translators last to reach the scene.

SCENES IN JANUARY

1
Waking to

a field of grassheads
strung with frail white lines.
Cat's cradled, sagging cups of dew.

Long nights

we gave to dream, to question.
Tall snapped pines (a whirling wind),
a few snow-isolated lights.

Hillside mist,

our coffees smoking, the window
angled onto melancholy trees.
A quiet to leave all words behind.

The little

that had promised so much more.
A week of filmy half-light,
harmonies like snowflakes falling through.

Remembering

the hooded man we saw in shadow.
Papers rippling in an open, sleek black case.
Remembering the fall...

2
A curl of flame

midway between the ice-damned
tributary and skyline grey.
The distances we have no time to close.

Small figures

tracking smoke downwind,
to where a cabin floats on white.
Faint lilt of voices, consonance of hope.

The railside generator
> hums, bright barriers swing down.
> A last look back, for what's beneath
> these new obliterating snows.

Reflecting steel,
> the lines in parallel, as time
> draws out a firm ground bass.
> Dazed, at ease, we're carried smoothly on.

Between the car and train
> (next station down the line)
> three men in black, bouquets...
> Exchanges, unrequited grief.

FOUR SCENES

from unwritten plays

I
The upper half of a classroom.
A blackboard and series of tall, narrow windows
past which white clouds are racing.

Sounds of traffic, sporadically, sometime harsh.

No view of the lower half of the room is afforded,
thus no teacher and no pupils.

Voices, rapid, overriding and indefinite,
betray the presence of the class.

On the board just one word, PAUSE,
its capitals almost obscured
by chalkdust hanging in light.

II
It is late February, late in the day.
A red sun angles over furrowed land
which rises to an almost empty sky.

Two silhouettes are poised, one nearer, one further,
engaged ambiguously in either work or contemplation.

A minute's silence, almost endless,
is broken by the first signs of recognition,
a distant call and wave.

The two figures begin to converge
as the cast emerges left and right:
Minister, Drab, Soldier, and Clerk.

The evening star goes (shockingly) unobserved.

III
An inner room, but unenclosed.
In one corner two globes of light
are suspended at intervals.

Tier upon tier of books line the walls.
A secret order unrevealed by title, colour or size.

Cigarette smoke rises, fades before the topmost tier
and its shadows, almost out of reach.

A single character is present, motionless but engaged,
his silhouette bleached by the difficult hour.

The time seesaws.
The clock throughout strikes nothing but a single note.

IV
Footsteps fade beyond the long wall of a gallery.

The artist's works are hung on even white.
Dark mottled mauves and pinks, his massive rock forms
occupy no more than half the space.

'The rest is for the mind', the artist
subsequently will fail to say.
Throughout he keeps his distance,
yet, at all times, makes the crucial move.

More footsteps heard. Same weight and interval.
Again they fade away.
Conclusions may be safely drawn.

The emphasis is his.

DREAM TERRITORY

i.

Broken trees, white leprous slopes.
All movement aching upward, faces
void of any strain. A moon that
skips away, returns and skips away.

ii.

Rocks, and rocks fragmenting.
Lacework of memory and ice.
The silent crowd looks on.
Horizons holding back the sea.

iii.

A glade, three peacocks prancing.
An atmosphere of miracle.
Each time the shadow falls a voice.
Distinct but muffled bells.

iv.

A windscape, nothing to see.
No light, no dark. The brief, unbroken
contours of a moving mind.
Their hissing and sighing. Flow.

DREAM INTERIOR

A curtain feels the breeze where plains of dry, uninterrupted yellow cross the room. An image poised, four-square, above the sand appears to lose its definition in the haze.

A shadow-line lifts from the right to tilt the frame where an old man sits. His glass is close to hand, a gash of white that fountains from a jug no one can see.

White wings become his tablecloth, a blur that once knew greater turbulence, now stilled with words. Their mysteries intact: the wings are closed.

Forever moved to speak, the old man bows before the reticence of air. Both curtains trail through dust. His outstretched hand fades quickly where it seeks to hold.

DUSK

The clouds in all their levels settle
    for what they have.

The canvas, ready primed, lacks nothing
    but the hour.

And here's the painter, eyes closed,
    lost in thought.

Still flight, the ikon waits to draw
    the gleam.

JAPANESE APPROACHES

1. Painters

The *presentment of a noble thought*
inspired by landscape,
rather than the view;

elimination of such minor detail
as distracts the eye -
chief elements to have the say;

all contrast low,
a colour harmony so delicate
the eye by mere degrees

shifts to the central point.

2. Printmakers

By colour mass not line,
an even disposition, lucid calm,
the charm of ordered feeling.

In Hiroshige,
the tenderness of dawn and sunset,
half-light of an evening street...

(*his style endured but for a little while,*
two pupils only at his side)
...the beat of rain,

the studied silence of deep sorrow.

INGREDIENTS

Japanese printing

The mind, its needs,
        obedience of hand and eye,
        degrees of calm.

Soft cherrywood,
        incised, accepting every line
        the brush would indicate.

A pot of rice paste
        blended with a range
        of pigments into ink.

From mulberry-bark
        a tough, fine paper,
        damped and burnished with

a sheaf of bamboo leaf
        wrapped round
        a fibre coil. No pause.

The worked idea,
        transferred, peeled free
        to bathe in light.

A mind in waiting,
        with its shadows, keen
        obliquities of thought.

FLUTED VASE 1949/50

a rhythm of form
under one clear concept
Bernard Leach

Temmoku, its difficult black iron glaze, occasionally pitted, thinning out to chocolate where the ribs rise up and swell, before they quickly tip back in again to meet the rim.

Quiet gravity of polished stone on shadow. Here, offset to win the photograph: a stand of thistles, blue, whose chosen frost, still folded in the leaf, puts out its cold, a crackle over light.

PENINSULA

Cold Spring, a smoking sea from which we climb. A window clouds where tea is boiled and poured, black to the brim. Stone cottage with its stoneware cups;

a guidebook indicates which clay: both white and red, the chosen sites Towednack and St Erth. For more than thirty hours the fiercest heat applied. Accepted colour out of cobalt, copper, manganese and iron... How painters quickly learn.

The window stares on outcrops, boulders, screes of Cornish stone. The time is ours. We drink and talk through histories of mining, house and art, inhaling tenses filtered by the wind.

ATLANTIC POST

A shallow pool beside the house, suffused with blue, where water might be drawn. To shelter, groves of dark, tough-leafed perennials that take the salt. And here are memories of woods, locked tight in narrow valleys draining from the moor.

One deepset window angles for the tor, its stack of granite slabs. Another gleans down yellow slopes toward the wind, its scree of vowels. The eagles gone, their blunted pinnacles at dusk are wreathed with flame. Refraction in the mind;

one room's translations glow with cadmium and cobalt, ceruleum, gold. The canvasses run wall to wall, escape to wider contours, gather in. Thought welling from another room, decked out in linen, pale. Three candles for the desert fathers and the night.

PAGE

The cliff-face honeycombed, receiver of a hundred winds, abrasive light.
All measure lost where arid distances unsettle time.

The old words clinging where some hand makes out the niche - small
shadow with its vessel of clay, its broken books.

*They wandered in the wilderness in a desert way, they found no city of
habitation,* but shelter of a kind,

its violet light still blooming over dust. With dying winds the empty
page... And new words falling silently, unstoppably, on outlines in the
mind.

HEROIC LIVES

I

Throughout disorder there are those whose consciousness is waiting for particular light. We see them raised infrequently, their archetype and worth recovered only as the times demand. They do not make demands themselves, their lives no more than sacrifice to what has gone before. And even those about them quickly lose their grasp of what is real, make fiction of an unresisting hour. A kind of haunting's soon initiated. Present walks the past. Its faded flowers are gathered with a will, their scent pervading every trance-like move we make as we, in turn, become auxiliary to myth. Strange colours glow. A few of us may come to hold their hand, unconsciously to lead them where they're asked to go, make verse a brilliant adjunct to their rise.

II

And there are those whose pale, almost anonymous lives are nurtured secretly. Somewhere an undiscovered landscape calls and finds them, takes them from their day-to-day. What's left seems real in all particulars, but that which moves and speaks is little more than fiction. The face is nothing but the last shade added to a thousand shades of history. Identity, if one can call it that, is pared to this, an open face that masks a shift. While out beyond, on greener, broader slopes there's joy at their selection. Peoples gather with unusual gifts. There's so much there that's shared and knowingly. On levels starred with wild, extraordinary flowers, things start to coalesce. The ground they walk on firms. Untraceable, unseen, it takes them on, sure-footed, anywhere they go.

THE CROSSING

*These brevities that become the diary
of another's days*

THE CROSSING

from Sven Hedin's record
Geographical Journal, March 1898

April 10, 1895
Takla Makan, another desert,
'1001 Cities', dekken-dekka,
all under dunes. The plan
a crossing east to west.
A hunt for signs.

S.H. and porters (only 4),
8 camels, other beasts.
Supplies of food and water
(100 gal. in all). Making
for Khotan Daria. Under sun.

Mid-April
Progress only fair
to middling; brackish water
dug out here and there
while camel, sheep and hen,
(not man) look on.

April 23, 24
True desert reached
but windstorms blind
as sun pours through.
No surface sure, the underfoot
perpetual motion.

Rises of 300 ft.,
criss-crossing dunes whose
crests continually break free,
slip down to leeward.
Lethal. Patterns perfect.

Shadows open up and close
in heat; each day
the changes to be seen
*both on the left
and on the right.* (1)

April 26
Concern: the water short.
Between two dunes
a well dug clear through clay.
Some moisture 3 ft. down,
but 3ft. more it's dry.

2 cups a day each man.
For sheep and dogs a bowlful.
Camels go without,
apart from saddle straw.
Till further notice.

Clouds mass - just once -
and darken. Tentcloths ready,
fully stretched,
but left undrenched as light
rolls from the lip and spreads.

April 29
The camels, greasy-mouthed,
lap through the butter
till there's none.
The water nil, thieved
by a guide, predictably.

Dust gets in everywhere,
the eyelids soon ingrained.
Each night the sky
puts out a frost of stars.
a.m., no dew on any brow.

May 1
The porters swig on rancid oil
(the camels') and journey on.
Sven left to Chinese brandy, (2)
almost paralysed.
The bells drift out and fade.

3 miles made up somehow,
he finds the party helpless,
slumped on sand. Their cries
for Allah only as
he sets up camp to shade, revive.

Sheep blood (his last) suits none.
What camels leave, some take
with sugar, vinegar
till the evening sees them off;
not seen again.

Much left behind they'd keep.
By camel now (to save his strength)
till night's pitch-dark.
On foot with lantern then.
Just Sven plus two.

Islam, by midnight, done for,
left - a lamp to see by,
follow if and when he can.
One camel spent. And further
precious goods to dump.

All night they walk.
May 2, 11 a.m. Eyes burn
till sun turns daylight black.
A waiting game. Naked,
buried in sand, their clothes
stretched out across a spade.

6 p.m. to 1 a.m.
Surprised to tread on moonlight's
fine, pale yellow sand.
May 3. By morning they
"descried a green tamarisk"...
Needles to chew. Inhaling shade.

Evening brings them
"three fresh poplars"
where they fail in time
to dig a well,
but light a fire to see, be seen.
A beacon for Islam.

May 4
More sterile sand.
One saving tamarisk that cools.
By 7 p.m. Sven has to leave Kasim.
The first time.
1 a.m. and Kasim reappears.

May 5
A dark line, smudge
across a bright horizon:
the Khotan river, wooded banks.
Poor K. now dazed -
a poplar left to shield.

7 p.m.
Spade handle for a staff,
through woods,
"long distances on all fours",
across the moonlit river bed.
5 hours to make 2 miles.

Sven startled: a single duck
lifts clear of... water.
A precious pool
left stranded
where the bed runs deep.

Before he drinks, a ritual.
He takes his pulse,
notes 49 then drinks.
2 Swedish jackboots filled
to save Kasim.

Not cities now but food.
3 days, 2 nights their lives
depend on grass and tadpoles
till the shepherds loom.
And greetings ring through heat.

At sunset: recognitions,
inklings of a light
that dies right out.
A silhouetted hawk that climbs
to fade in gold...

Islam appears from nowhere,
tells how merchants found him,
leads their camel
packed with Chinese money,
instruments and notes.

(Much more in time turns up. (3)
Sven's cities:
images of Buddha,
painted walls and pillars...
A "second Sodom in the desert".)

To Kashgar first, a few returns.
Truth shimmering in the desert air.
2 men and 7 camels lost.
Cold ruins
anchored under drifting sand.

(1) *Tao Te Ching*
(2) "which otherwise was used for a lamp-stove"
(3) His second expedition

GRADIENTS

We cross the desert with some last remains
Of a former image in our minds
Giuseppe Ungaretti

GRADIENTS

I

POWERSAW

That special sound when the blade ripped through the final bark and out.
So good to hear. And the clearing, when he left it, ran with shining
dust like snow.

At nightfall, in his room, he held a glass and smiled. The weight, the
faint vibration of the saw still lingered in his hands.

Each sip he took ran through him with its cold. The room was quiet.
Tomorrow lay so far away across the hills: another camp, dark swathes
of pine. But not for him. Like a connoisseur he tongued the first
meltwater of the Spring.

GRADIENTS

In travelling he found himself at home, quick to relax in green or darker
contours, miles from anywhere. The shimmering of lights in carriages,
reflections, those mazy tricklings of rain were now predictable. Each
journey took him back through foreign fields he'd known, the white and
interlocking crosses of the dead.

He seldom spoke, not even querying the odd unscheduled stops. But
falling tones and the long black rush through tunnels were always an
excuse. He welcomed their excitement like the unexpected friend.
Trackside or overhead, like arteries, the endless cables surged with
power.

EXPATRIATE

A glow, a haze. Something filling one end of a room, almost yellow.
He remembered sitting there the previous night, quite alone. The colour
and its volume holding him. No words or thoughts had come, no pain.

Now he wrung his hands and searched the wavelengths for a voice. A sound he'd held despite the years. Still clear. Light, crisp-edged, a little foreign at the point where consonant ran into vowel...

Meticulous in his usual way, re-tuning back through static to the faintest waver. The needle all but dead, crossing a thousand frequencies. An hour or so, then something like despair as he put the headphones down. The atmosphere all wrong.

Recovering, he found his eyes had fixed on a gleam where the curtain ran its hem through dust. Red tiles, real red: their hidden warmth. And he rose a little stiffly, anxious for the touch.

No guarantee the signals would improve. Too many hours till dusk... And he watched the morning light strike through the faded, half-drawn curtains, touching his lamp-shade, almost awakening its sympathetic yellow, filling out the day.

HALO

After eleven years he could hardly be surprised. The brass was pitted everywhere, each black speck and its faint penumbra impossible to clean. The lacquer, he had told her then, was sacrilege - no saving in the end of anybody's time.

Lifting the oval frame from the wall, he saw how much was lost - the absence of her portrait taking even his identity away. The ill-lit room was anyone's. He stared for minutes at the cold, emulsioned wall.

Before he climbed the steps again, he paused to look more closely at her smile, surprised to find how firm, how unselfconscious it appeared. The more he looked, the less it seemed she'd once been his.

The picture back, he seemed to recognise his place, his role. In future he would try to spend more time with her. The tarnished frame would have to wait, even that haloing of dust he'd missed in his dismay.

ROUND

Deep green, and how the skins all gleamed. Not now, he walked right past the dish and turned, a song still troubling him...

Not that he'd never hummed the tune before. He had, and frequently, but that was years ago. Surely the cause lay somewhere in a dream. Last night... Last night was out of reach - place, person and event - and yet a faint emotion flickered somewhere in his mind.

Melancholy. Like the placid waters of his childhood, winter sunlight, the voices of his family... It seemed the list went on and on. How all-inclusive was this melancholy, how costly of his time.

The apples swam back into view. He counted them, observed their roundness, feeling each and imagining the tart, singular flavour which was his choice. At once he bit his lip, knowing the song was parody. If that page wasn't filled tonight, the scissors used decisively... He broke into a run.

AFTER THE STORM

On the tide-wet, shelving stones he was not alone. The others, hunch-backed, kicked and scuffed their way methodically along the shore: the real beachcombers with their sticks and bags...

In the smoky, morning light he prised free from the wrack a small chipped block of tourmaline, a cork float, wafer thin, a lens of pale green glass... then threw them to the wave. His friends would hear how mediocre were the pickings after such a storm, after this night of wrecks and loss.

There was a time the pieces would have gleamed for him. Not now. And anyway, he had such little room to spare. After an hour he walked away, half-satisfied. At least he knew what wasn't there, what in a trice would raise his fierce imagination to a blaze.

SKEINS

His aerial absorbed the dusk and shone with a pinkish light. Plant-like, its slender frame climbed high above the house, quivering in a stream of air. At a window he watched and waited for the days, their cloudless skies, while distant skeins of geese, like dark beads, headed out across the hills.

Sometimes his children came to mind, their wild impressive movements on the land. And then regret: those childhood stories he had failed to tell, those *matters* that would put down roots. Instead, there were days he'd given over to the sun, crazy days when all they'd do was play...

Now this little, growing cloud to watch, its dark shape changing as it moved his way. Unravelling. Then: one, two, three... the dark birds settling quickly on his aerial, straightening their wings, their raucous conversation bringing out his smile. How far he'd come. How many languages he'd learned.

THE GULL

The sky was an off-white blur. He couldn't hear the wind. Not a rooftop showed its steady stream. He sat for minutes puzzled at the calm, the morning rinsed of sound. His prayer was plain: too many days lacked intervals of colour, a shape he could discern. So much was alien.

When he saw it, the gull was almost motionless in space: just now and then a tilt, a righting, head into the wind. So close he guessed its very bulk between his hands. When he edged the window open just an inch, it took his breath away. A cool wind there and scouring... His few unbroken words approved.

After a batch of letters there were all those old plans he would resurrect, revise. The hours flew. By nightfall he was overtired and almost mesmerised by the words he'd penned. He couldn't lose that image of the gull. A glint of orange in its staring eye, one feather lifting as, continually, it screamed and climbed away.

MIGRAINE

A steady, high-pitched buzz, faint but insistent. It reached him all day long across the town.

A dark workshop: one narrow window, a single bulb. And the two men who chiselled, cut and gouged, understanding its special calm, its warmth.

He'd been there sometimes but never stayed - a simple job he wanted done, some casual words. In his attic room he remembered how each length of wood ran at the saw to separate in swirls of dust. He saw the gleam of moving steel.

Empty-handed still, everything he ever wanted laid out neatly in his flat... He felt his temple - another thrill of pain. He knew he'd not be free for long.

At times like these the walls he'd painted in the Spring seemed far too pale. How easily he'd settled for the light, its constant searching, openness. The four walls shone. He saw himself bleach smoothly into them.

SHELTER

The hollow would be perfect, surely. He raced for its smoothly weathered red...

...finding what he had not seen before: a curtain of stiff and ancient roots that searched the entrance roughly, blindly in the changing light.

Above him the tree was frozen, helpless, in the act of falling, not quite bridging the narrow lane. There was time enough to see its dying power before rain swept across the hill.

The sword in the stone, he thought. Again.

And he gripped and cursed the roots, but they wouldn't budge. Dark sandstone somewhere trickled free. What could he do? His diaries, filled with parallels, coincidence and mystery, seemed all so out of date. The skies were racing now.

Split the wood, lift the stone...

All he could tell of the dusty hollow was someone's childhood - dry, serene. The tree, the house would never fall. But why? Wasn't this the rain inside his shirt, his shoes?

When the lightning flashed, his face, turned upward, was a pale unseeing ochre and everything was, as it should be, in its place.

II

FEVER

I must have been delirious for hours...
All those old voices, distant voices from the past. A cold, dark well,
its echoing. And brilliance, the brilliance of water that you find half in,
half out of light. My aching eyes could not hold on: I held them tight.

So many folk all gathered round me. I couldn't tell if I or they were
travelling. Like strange new suns we spun against the charcoal glare of
space. Then everything was pieces, fragments of ourselves, a rain of
dust...

One voice I know I moved towards before I woke. I recognised it
instantly, the way it called, but knew it didn't call for me. The voice
was mine.

THE HISTORIAN

'His room was high. The window opening, as he'd said, upon unusual
distances. Reflections, too, if one took his chair: the forecast cloud now
gliding from the west, broad charcoal roofs. All else was shadow and
dusky green.

On the sill his book lay open to the light: a book of sacred groves and
ritual enclosures. On the left-hand page were countless diagrams in
minature of *viereckschanzen* in Bavaria and France.

Only the book was out of place. Elsewhere the room was tidy - one
might say immaculate. A quiet man, I could almost hear her say. He
gave his life to history... Barely a wave when he left, apparently.
Almost routine.

I handed her the private papers, details of arrangements he'd already
made. At the door the air was bitter. There was nothing to be said.
Pehaps, in time, the matter of his green cord suit, a solicitor's
astonishment, an oak tree in a distant field.'

AFTER DUSK

Too long this walk without my friends. Dark lanes criss-crossing an
open countryside. On either side those massive banks of bramble, rich
red earth. Only a narrow strip of sky between.

A fine, warm night and one I'll need to keep with me. We'd shared our
last meal, said goodbye and started home, the whole world on our
minds.

A week in which we'd sought and found the Perseids, admired their
fierce return: my diary crammed with notes. This night ill-starred, so
much shut out, the people of the constellations lost from view.

EVENINGS

This, perhaps, was how it always was. Late Summer evenings, the
children shrill across the beach. I've walked along and now beyond this
waterline, knowing by heart its soft, repeating crash.

So many small dark arms, their rapid jerk and whirl. Each stone
invisible as the racing eyes.

I make no mention of the intervals, their clarity. Instead I wait, look
out and down, perfecting words to greet the fall. A vivid flash each time
a new stone hits the swell.

EXCHANGES

That *Life of Schubert* , its clear line drawings teasing me. I couldn't
count the likenesses. Perhaps the giver saw them too. One Christmas
years ago. And where is she?

Mayrhofer, Vogl, von Spaun and others round you in the Vienna
streets, singing and spinning the money out. Between your illnesses.
The music in you almost impossible to contain. So short a life...

Red cloth and crisp white pages, quarto size. A handsome book and one of many, foolishly, I came to lose. How they've been missed. Those treasures - our lives I mean, dear Franz - we should have grown into and saved.

TITLE

I was remembered for little, it seems. For strange, uncertain hours and moves. My injuries perhaps, those I'd confessed...

Words gathered, looked to rearrange. Somewhere my Persian gave himself to cool reflections in a dusty pane. The tides receded and returned. In corners, between their delicate constructions, the spiders paused, came nervously to rest.